# ACTA

Acta
©Patrick Wilcox / Cathexis Northwest Press

No part of this book may be reproduced without written permission of the
publisher or author, except in reviews and articles.

First Printing: 2023

ISBN: 978-1-952869-83-9


Editing & Design by C. M. Tollefson
Cathexis Northwest Press

cathexisnorthwestpress.com

# ACTA

### POEMS BY
## PATRICK WILCOX

*Cathexis Northwest Press*

*This book is for Kara, my first and best reader.*

# Table of Contents

# I

In the beginning we thought we knew what we were making. We thought because the foundation was salt & stone & laced with the last of the old world's rebar that the acta would stand cogent longer than the remaining eras we kept tucked away in our back pockets. We were making *progress*.

We thought because the gears were numberless, their teeth coupled close as night, that when we flipped its switch the acta would ignite & whir & do what we could not. We were making *necessity*. [Give us weather acta] we asked & the acta spun & spat deafening san serif into the sky. We added hatches with thick hinges to better access its inner workings, brought our children to revel at its face.

We asked [give us sport acta] & the acta rolled, swiveled, rumbled & bowed. We were making *certainty*. In the beginning the acta moved as worms moved. We stayed gaze-arrested for years. Weeds cracked through the foundation, ensnared the acta's four bolted feet. Miles of barbed vine embraced its sides.

We added sleek touch screens & pixels inside of pixels inside of pixels so we would know what we saw was sharp & true. [*Give us traffic acta*] [*dog bite acta*] [*bicentennialacta*][*celebritybirthdayacta*] [*sunsetskycamacta*][*newfilmreleaseacta*] & the acta bellowed, boasted & pruned its paint & left only a few of its favorite corporate decals.

In the beginning we thought we knew what the acta meant when it sent us color & sound--so when the acta began to convulse, stammer, quiver & clot, we threw ourselves on its back to settle its seizure. Our fingers cramped & bled & in time we let go. [*Give us murder acta*] we asked & language-lacquered plumes became our sky. We were making *autonomy* beyond *autonomy*.

Please believe us when we say there was nothing we could do once the acta, with a deep green breath & steely heave through a mouth we never gave it, finally spoke. [*You should be terrified*] the acta said [*You should be happy*].

# Coronavirus world map: tracking the spread of the outbreak

Buckshot with red spots, our world limps
into autumn. If I look at the map on the TV
close enough I can see America. When I press

my nose to the screen I can see Illinois. Press harder
and there is Chicago. And look, in this pixel,
my apartment and whatever is left of me staring

at a map of a world whose name I once knew. Trees
flutter in the wind and cars crash into them the same
way they used to. Red spots punctuate the stretched

skin between my fingers and inch around the backs
of my hands, up my forearms. After I totaled my car
into an oak tree, I called my sister, begged her

for providence. I shouldn't be alone. I can't stop prodding
the news anchor. My TV screen is cracking. Red spots
punctuate the backs of my knees, my withering

thighs. Red spots punctuate the days. I see you
there through this window of a page. I am
in your home. I am in your head. I am everywhere,

all the time, all at once. My sister
won't find me for weeks. When she comes
to check on me and must break down

the door she will see the spotted
pattern of this new world, her eyes
wide as a breaking headline.

# Here's how the Enhanced Fujita Scale works, and this is what it looks like

Before the dogs barked back
at the train-like call, before
            dead-clover sky

between street lamps,
before a tree's rooty bottom
jutted from the top of St. Marks
like some envious answer
            to the steeple,

and roofs were licked shingle-clean,
toilet seats necklaced bird feeders,
clawfoot bathtubs lay beached
in backyards, before the funeral home
pirouetted up and out, sending my body,
two days dead, into the windshield of a girl
            I loved in high school,

where were we before this?
When they trace the twister's trail
they will only see you
            and I

and this new exposure
all poised mid-collision. They will study
each home, how each home
            sulks, torn open

like a doll's house, leaning
on the east, like me, half-naked
and vulnerable and they will, by day's end,
report back how every moment to follow
            threatens to carry us away.

# Florida man washes ashore after trying to walk on water to New York

Florida Man, equipped with straw hat
and stilts, wades between the wave-broken

beach rock closer to the tidal horizon. The coast
always begs him to go everywhere

he has never been. Behind Florida Man, other
elderly residents of North Bay Retirement Center

repaint sun-baked housing pastel blue
and orange and green and red. They clean

sand from hapless porches. *Where have you
been?* the elderly ask. If Florida Man chooses

the Atlantic he will leave behind his bedside
collection of cough drops, sea shells,

and photographs of dead relatives: ten distant
cousins, three brothers, a wife, another wife,

a son. His pockets are empty. He wades past
the pier, past the port's final warning buoy:

*here is your Florida Man, your old and dying
and nameless man on stilts bridging*

*the longest stretch of water, risking abduction
by waves into the endless pull of ocean.*

# Does this headline look blue to you? Then it might also feel like a triangle: Research shows that synesthesia may extend in more directions than we thought

I know the number one
    is red and five is red

wine and six is white. I know white
is grime under nails. I know science
    is green and history

is blue and blue is night's tepid
    green whisper. But what do you hear

when you taste
my kiss? What do you taste
    when your history

holds mine?
    I know my body

is a sieve
through which the world strains
    what it wants

from what it does not. I know your body
    is a dead language

born again, discovering
its hands, spouting
    words that mean nothing

and everything. I know a circle
    is what's left unsaid at dinner, or the heft

of winter's treeline charred
by savage dusk. I know all glass
    is broken glass and like music

these shards lay flickering
        around our bare feet. I know the lullaby

your fingertips sing
across the back of my neck
        and I know its lyrics

are our secret names
        kept hidden so long

we forgot where
we put them. I know every moment
        is a mile, how we spent miles

swaying over that broken glass,
        not feeling a thing until I know I don't know

the story my lips tell
        your morning shoulder. I hope it's the one

where summer never ends.

# Firefighter killed in California wildfire sparked by gender reveal party

A city worker wipes bird droppings off the monuments
of men who built this town. Off the lips of dead fountains,
sculpted grey stags and children. Off the towns people
who have perched here for decades aching for water to spit

into a basin. Cracks cross sidewalks
like severed faults. Weeds reach through like the arms
of farmers, their combines made vacant. The new
millenia marked the last reporting of:

clouds, cold, talk, fathers, winter, rain, shade and brought
the beginning of perpetual day. Thirst is a currency,
sleep a false reprieve. Town Hall is condemned. Its steps
haggardly chipped like a coastal rock jetty.

Light ignites along the horizon. Those who look
wonder if the sun is rising or setting or if the surrounding
fields have burnt up. If allowed a question, I might ask:
Where have the birds gone? Can the widow

on Sweet Briar cross her farm, touch her dog
sprawled out sideways and feel it breathe? Where
is winter? Where is the cigarette-battered voice
cooing with the salted wind? Come home. Enter quietly

at two A.M. Bring words and soft light. When you leave
take me with you. Make me think you never left.

# Tracing the expanding definition of fatherhood

My son's needy palm passes
            through a blade

of sunlight. One day
            my son will hold it.

He will use it
            against me.

# City approves demolition of library

We waited for everything
to come down
      on top of itself. We waited

with all the others
along the sidewalk. The library,
      our first words, first kiss,

now condemned, waited too. *Tell me*
*something meaningless*, she begged, nosing
      into my chest. I said, *40,000 Americans*

*are injured each year*
*by toilets. Like finger tips,*
      *everyone's tongue print*

*is different. No word in the English language*
*rhymes with orange, month, silver,*
      *or purple. An ostrich's eye*

*is bigger than its brain.* The library collapsed
into itself, thousands of brick-abandoned
      kisses, and the gunshot pops just before

might as well have come
from inside us. *In France it is legal to marry*
      *a dead person.*

          ***

The night before our ceremony,
I snuck into his room. He said
      he never felt so sure,

but his kiss collapsed
into itself. *Tell me something*
      *meaningless*, he begged,

pressing his forehead
to mine. I said, *a cockroach*
        *can live weeks without its head*

*before starving to death. Ketchup*
*was sold in the 1830s*
        *as medicine. The electric chair*

*was invented by a dentist. The average*
*lead pencil can draw a line*
        *35 miles long.* I left the room,

but could see down the hall
a splinter of light remained
        beneath the door until 3 AM. *The Nile*

*crocodile can hold its breath underwater*
*for nearly two hours while waiting*
        *to strike prey.*

                    \*\*\*

We had no business pretending
we ever knew the hidden cogs
        of a heart. But we kissed each other

goodbye each morning anyway. Nobody
believed we could be anything
        but careless, never-ending

in love. Even in the hospital, surrounded
by nurses, her body slowly, inevitably
        splitting open: *It would take a hundred earths*

*filed end to end to stretch across the face*
*of the sun. Jellyfish have no brains, no bones,*
        *no heart. There are no clocks in Las Vegas*

casinos. You were born and we were stranded
on the moon. *Bees sometimes sting other bees*
        *without reason.*

                    \*\*\*

You were a burden
we could not live without. Most nights
       I thought my love

would kill you. Most nights
you cried. When you were quiet,
       I watched you like the dark between streetlamps

just to see you breathe. *Water*
*makes different sounds pouring*
       *depending on its temperature. For a hundred years,*

*maps have shown an island*
*that doesn't exist. People break up*
       *most often on Mondays.* Bed springs

choked under the weight. The crib cries
in the next room might as well have come
       from inside us. *Nearly all species*

*to have ever lived on Earth*
       *are now extinct.*

            \*\*\*


We sat for weeks in the love-light
snow, your pacifier in her pocket,
       your lab results in mine. *Banging your head*

*against the wall burns 150 calories per hour. Peanuts*
*are an ingredient in dynamite. Any pair of languages*
       *have a common ancestor.* It's impossible

what can happen
in two years, two months,
       two minutes. The shouts from the couple

across the street might as well have come
from inside us. *Viking kings were buried*
       *in their ships, set adrift to fog and sea.*

            \*\*\*

We buried you in autumn encircled
by lilacs and crabgrass. I found her in your room curled
        beside the crib in a question mark trying to speak

a language we never really could. *Every time you shuffle*
*a deck of cards you get a combination*
        *that has never been.* Like the plumbing trap beneath the sink,

I thought I could fix her myself. I opened her up
while she was sleeping without knowing the true names
        of parts. Gears and springs too small to hold

collapsed like words in a hospital waiting room. I could not see
how they wanted to work and only managed
        to break her further. And of course, she was never

really sleeping, but hoped my meddling
might work by accident. *What of tomorrow?* She asked,
        *the next day and the next?* I pressed

my forehead to hers. *The calcium*
*in our bones, the iron in our blood, the breath*
        *in our brick-abandoned kisses*

*were stolen from dying stars,*
*from their never-ending*
                *bygone explosions.*

# Covering West Virginia's long history of broken promises

Our last quiet year and it's raining. A cemetery built on a hillside
    has been -- for decades on top of decades --

forgotten until the unforgiving rush
    of raindrops relax the earth like tiny blue pills relax

the body and the hillside set back its head, let down
    its shoulders, and bled. The hillside bled

bodies, confederates and yankees, bled lovers and morning
    dew, mothers, their children and rolls over-stuffed

with pepperoni and cheese, bled gravel roads, their lift
    and their let go, forever winding and unwinding

through Green Ash and River Birch and Black Willow, bled salt
    and timber, bled houses coughing, clutching its hillside

and the hillside clutching its houses, their unchained
    yard dogs and cinderblock-propped trucks and sheet metal

shacks all to its chest like bibles, bled empty coal mines
    and drunken cigarette smoke semaphores, bled the vacant

storefronts that said they love you, the Chokecherry shrubs
    that said they love you

        and now -- as always -- the hillside looks away

    from what it once had and -- as always --

        the rain

            dies in the night.

# II

How dare you look at us like that.
You were not there. We opened the
hatches, exchanged knowing glances at
the automated guts we no longer
understood. We severed the plugs
from each battery, yanked wires

[*Give us cancer acta*]

& vines by the fistful from its ribs,
but the acta wouldn't stop spewing its
sticky ink. The principles that kept it
running

[*You should be happy*]

did not belong to us anymore. We
shattered like dropped glass in every
direction. The acta found us & with its
many hands drug us back, lifted us up
by the heel level to our new black sky.
There was no heart

[*Give us murder acta*]

only mire & madness and what must
be done so the acta dropped us into
its bleak maw, swallowed us whole. We
slid down unable to dig in our nails.
We slid

[*You should be terrified*]

past money stacks embezzled while
the city water soured, past a wildfire
and the town it wanted to love the
only way it knew how, past a gas
station, a boy, and a bullet. We gave
credence to blowhards, algorithms,

*[More, more murder acta]*

grifters & lesser voices made loud by pseudoscience. We panhandled for callous words shed by silhouettes & social slugs in tinfoil hats, realized too late that the shadow cast over this cold history would not be our own. We filled the acta with so much of us, stuffing

*[You should be happy]*

its ever-starving stomach. The walls stretched & ached & stretched & burst. There was so much of us. Like a bullet the acta sent us

from its bolt-backed chamber

all the way home.

# Six killed in interstate chain pileup outside Flagstaff

We spent entire lifetimes wondering
what wounds looked like when not beaten back
by headlights, why they begged for blood
and more deft blood, who they wrote

their last love letters to. Every billboard I've seen
along the highway could not escape the pinch
of my forefinger and thumb. If I couldn't have you
I would settle for half-drunk phone calls

cast over the ever-healing bruise
of midnight. Every town we've sped through
was ours in a past life. I spent entire lifetimes
trying and failing to hold you closer. Every night

I tried to stitch our bodies together
but only left them roadkill along the earthwork
of what had once been a horizon, something
worth a picture untaken. Remember that night

 we didn't dance in Kansas? We bled out just enough
language so that there was no word for *love*

or *loneliness*, just measure
             and more pale measure beating

and beating
             and beating. Remember

those midnight miles we didn't open our eyes
             through Virginia? We spun out in the fog

of our own lackluster, crossing country
and more akimbo country. We guessed

which way, just past the hilltop, our road
             would break. Left or right, it never

really mattered. I shouldn't have,
            like all those tiny billboards,

tried to keep you. All the miles we have
            before home

couldn't wake us up. With only
our bodies we inked

            onto real maps

                        unreal highways.

# Pretty words: looking for melodic combinations

*Cellar Door.* Two words proven, through the science
of sound and sadness, to be the most beautiful phrase
in the English language. Say them now, loud
to your own unfamiliar reflection. *Cellar
door. Cellar door.* Two words stuffed, once sewn together,
      with unbearable meanings not fit

for dinner table talk. *Cellar door.* But what of our
other options? Let's begin with *just come home.*
Whisper it, will you now, into the hollowed-out
cool of your pillow. Yes, j*ust come
home,* flat as Kansas or the small
      of her back. *Just come home.* Or,

I suppose, *rollercoaster.* Smooth as porcelain
and just as delighted to break. Slip it
into the next annual telephone conversation
you have with your father
      about regret. But what

of *stalled car*? What of *stopped short*
or *deathbed back sore*? Where on such a scale
might these words drop, burst, and plume
like epiphany? Let's consider
for a moment the likelihood
      of *not right now* or *not so*

soon or *not at all.* Let's consider the likelihood
that the most beautiful sound in English
is the emptiness before impact, unborn
and strung up like an ornament
in all that space
      between us.

# Summer of racial reckoning

No, we can do better -- That summer
was so much more -- Summer

of swelter. Summer of sickness
and last ditch efforts -- Starving

young summer of lost music
notes -- Summer of notes stacked

on notes that became song -- Summer
of bullet and blood -- Staccato

summer of hope -- Summer of rally
and riot -- Hysterical summer

of hope unheard. Summer of song
and brick and glass -- Summer

of consumption -- Half-forgotten summer
of fire -- Unsung summer

we all watched the life leave a man
under the weight of a knee -- Brambled

summer of tear gas and midnight amber
we will rename until we name it right.

# How to keep a relationship alive, according to experts

One night, five weeks after your funeral
you crawled out of your grave. You crept
across barren streets and gutters half full
with autumn, dragging your legs and losing bits
of belly with each block. I didn't hear your gritty,
      ceaseless groan when you struggled

through the open window, when you writhed
down the hallway, or at last when you snuck
into my bed. The lack of color that spills
through any given night, spilled through you
completely. The morning after your return I fried
      bacon and eggs neither of us ate. I told you

I missed you because once, back when
the moon could still speak to me, we drove
north and held hands across a hundred
songs and at your wake I slipped their lyrics
inside your suit pocket. After breakfast
      I combed the maggots out of your beard

and took you to my parent's new house
for dinner. My father asked about last winter
and you didn't answer. I took you out for drinks
with friends uptown. They asked if we cared
to buy back all the songs we thought were ours
      and you didn't answer. We drank too much

and you drove us home. Guilt crawls
like a body out of its grave. Tonight
when we crawl into bed, you will ask
if there is anything I need, anything I want,

               anything at all,

     and I will answer,

         *sleep.*

# Photos: Chaos erupts as pro-Trump mob storms the Capitol

Two black gleaming buses parked beneath a dark pink sky. In one windshield reflection: the Capitol. Morning sun has painted it gold.

A field of red hats and American flags. Four people improve their view atop porta johns. They are cold.

A bearded man adorned in fur and horns holds a sign stating *Q SENT ME*. His face is painted red, white, and blue. He is America.

Too many flags to count, on stage and off. A field of hats and flags without limitations. Trump is speaking on stage. Even in the silence of a picture his words ring deafening.

A man in a gas mask walks along the sidewalk. He holds a large flag and pole against his chest like a rifle.

Makeshift gallows frame the Capitol's rotunda and dome. A noose swings in the wind. It wants to fulfill its purpose.

In the foreground: a skewed confederate flag. In the background: a woman wears Prada sunglasses and holds up a crucifix. The crucifix asks a dozen questions, none of which concern God.

Seven regular people scale a wall leading to the Capitol entrance. When they reach the top, they become something else.

A man batters a riot shield into a window. He is smiling. The window relents. The officer who once held the riot shield is out of frame, on the ground, screaming while being trampled. He is certain he will die.

A man wearing a charcoal suit and patriotic mask faces the camera. His arms are stretched out between a door frame. People duck under, rushing into the Capitol. Smoke whips in grand circles.

Desks, tables, and chairs are heaped against a door to the House Chamber where electoral votes are being counted. Three officers in suits have guns pointed at the barricade. One representative has a sign asking the rioters to stop.

Night blankets the Capitol. The long bright fire of an ammunition explosion silhouettes a thousand people. They scream and beg for truth only they can know.

# Man on hospital bed sends internet into meltdown as he turns out to be a cake

I lied
    because you lied

and never would
    have loved me

had you known
    what I always was.

# Algorithm helps New York decide who goes free before trial

The courthouse that calls to me
     is only five blocks from home
but I drive anyway and you

are shirtless on the corner, the rain

and your skin each terrified of the other. The light
     stays red long enough for you to ask
for a lift and maybe I'll drop you

off at the plasma center

or maybe I won't. Maybe you'll ask
     to bum a cigarette
or pull a knife on me

and I'll have no choice but to kill you. Maybe

we will ride getaway together, speed through a school
     zone, take every billboard into our palms, clench,
crumble, and spread their remains

over the 1950s. We will set fire to a Bentley

and all of language, murder
     a store clerk with memory and sink his body
        in the river. They already know. Maybe

     they will lock us in a ward, make us

case study subjects of fathers
     without fathers. Maybe we will rob
the city block of blue and give every bit back

to prayer logic.  Maybe we will call home

and someone will answer. They already know
     of all those burnt out cars,
        all those bodies in the river,

all those hollow words

        for which we'll hang. They already know
    and hope they have no choice
but to keep us cuffed

    to all the crimes we must commit.

# 10 things estate sales won't tell you

When the phone rang I thought, *this is it*. One last
late night porch light smoke. One last dawn torn

open by sunrise. And again, when the car
pulled up. One last morning

news report. One last broken breakfast dish. One last
look into empty attic boxes. And again, when you spoke

through a knock on the door. One last
spilled drink. And again, and again, and again

when I answered with a glance
through the peephole. *This is it*. One last

memory lapse. One last lost voice. One last

spilled song
     empty song
          dawn song
               odd song.

And finally, when you waited
in the doorway, perched
      like a crow on a power line.
          One last beginning.

# III

We were *certainty, progress,*
           & *necessity.* We were *autonomy*

beyond *autonomy.* We were falling,
           flying, turning over

& over like a cadence
           in the heart of a god. We were ink

in a sky possessed, pixels
           on a screen skewed. Today

your money is made
           & unmade. Today, a fire breaks

into your home. Today
           a bullet shoots through your kitchen

through your shopping mall
           through your classroom

through your yesterday
           and into your body

which makes it no longer
           your body. After we felt

our bodies kiss the ground
           we managed enough strength

to rise to our hands & knees
           & calm our breath. We carried

the acta in pieces to a swatch
           of earth at the edge of time, the place

we bury our dead, where
           we know just enough

to get ourselves into trouble
           when it comes

to atomic daydreams

           like guilt, hope

& resurrection.

# Acknowledgments

All my gratitude to family and friends who have lent me their unwavering support and encouragement when I needed it most.

Also, many thanks to the faculty and students at the University of Central Missouri where several of these poems were first workshopped and made exponentially better.

It's important to note the titles of these poems are headlines borrowed from various media outlets and the body of the poems themselves do not reflect beliefs of the corresponding organizations. The outlets are listed below as well as the literary journals that first gave a handful of these poems a chance.

And finally, I want to thank C.M. Tollefson and Cathexis Northwest Press for bringing my book into the world. Their patience and guidance throughout the publishing process have been a great comfort to me."

"10 things estate sales won't tell you"
Headline from *Market Watch* // 19 June 2013
Published by *Cathexis Northwest Press*

"Algorithm helps New York decide who goes free before trial"
Headline from *The Wall Street Journal* // 20 September 2020
Published in *Bangalore Review*

"City approves demolition of library"
Headline from *Tampa Bay Times* // 3 September 2005
Published in *The MacGuffin*

"Coronavirus world map: tracking the spread of the outbreak"
Headline from *National Public Radio* // 3 March 2020
Published in *Maudlin House*

"Covering West Virginia's long history of broken promises"
Headline from *ProPublica* // 27 April 2018
Published in *West Trade Review*

"Does this headline look blue to you? Then it might also feel like a triangle: Research shows that synesthesia may extend in more directions than we thought"
Headline from *HuffPost* // 17 September 2016

"Florida man washes ashore after trying to walk on water to New York" Headline from *ABC News* // 27 July 2021
Published by *Drunk Monkeys*

"Here's how the Enhanced Fujita Scale works, and this is what it looks like"
Headline from *Smithsonian Magazine* // 23 May 2013
Published in *Quarter After Eight*

"Firefighter killed in California wildfire sparked by gender reveal party"
Headline from *National Public Radio* // 18 September 2020
Published in *Arcade Magazine*

"How to keep a relationship alive, according to experts"
Headline from *Brides Magazine* // 24 June 2021
Published by *Midway Journal*

"Man on hospital bed sends internet into meltdown when he turns out to be cake"
Headline from *Daily Star* // 18 February 2021
Published in *The Dillydoun Review*

"Photos: chaos erupts as pro-Trump mob storms the Capitol"
Headline from *NBC News* // 7 January 2021

"Pretty words: looking for melodic combinations"
Headline from *Winston-Salem Journal* // 4 April 2010

"Six killed in interstate chain pile up outside of Flagstaff"
Headline from *Associated Press* // 1989
Published by *Cathexis Northwest Press*

"Summer of racial reckoning"
Headline from *National Public Radio* // 16 August 2020
Published in *Lighthouse Weekly*

"Tracing the expanding definition of fatherhood"
Headline from *National Public Radio* // 14 June 2019
Published in *Vineyard Literary*

Patrick Wilcox is from Independence, Missouri, a large suburb just outside Kansas City. He studied English and Creative writing at the University of Central Missouri where he also was an Assistant Editor for Pleiades and Editor-in-Chief of Arcade. He is a three-time recipient of the David Baker Award for Poetry, the 2020 honorable mention of Ninth Letter's Literary Award in Poetry, and grand-prize winner of The MacGuffin's Poet Hunt 26. His work has appeared in Maudlin House, Quarter After Eight, Bangalore, and West Trade Review, among others. He currently teaches English Language Arts at William Chrisman High School.

# Also Available
## from
## Cathexis Northwest Press:

Vanity Unfair and Other Poems
by Robert Eugene Rubino

Destructive Heresies
by Milo E. Gorgevska

Bodies of Separation
by Chim Sher Ting

The Night with James Dean and Other Prose Poems
by Allison A. deFreese

About Time
by Julie Benesh

Suspended
by Ellen White Rook

The Unempty Spaces Between
by Louis Efron

Quomodo probatur in conflatorio
by Nick Roberts

Call Me Not Ishmael but the Sea
by J. Martin Daughtry

Coming To Terms
by Peter Sagnella

Wild Evolution
by Naomi Leimsider

Honeymoon Shoes
by Valyntina Grenier

Practising Ascending
by Nadine Hitchiner

*Cathexis Northwest Press*

Printed in the USA
CPSIA information can be obtained
at www.ICGtesting.com
LVHW040806060923
757193LV00006B/143